AF228634

GIRLS' LACROSSE

By Brendan Flynn

SportsZone

An Imprint of Abdo Publishing
abdobooks.com

abdobooks.com

Published by Abdo Publishing, a division of ABDO, PO Box 398166, Minneapolis, Minnesota 55439. Copyright © 2022 by Abdo Consulting Group, Inc. International copyrights reserved in all countries. No part of this book may be reproduced in any form without written permission from the publisher. SportsZone™ is a trademark and logo of Abdo Publishing.

Printed in the United States of America, North Mankato, Minnesota.
102021
012022

Cover Photo: Rich Barnes/Cal Sport Media/Zuma Wire/AP Images
Interior Photos: Rich Barnes/Cal Sport Media/AP Images, 4–5, 7, 26, 41; Patrick Smith/Getty Images Sport/Getty Images, 10, 20–21, 36–37; Stony Brook Athletics, 12–13, 17; Alex Cena/NCAA Photos/Getty Images, 15, 33; Rich Barnes/Cal Sport Media/Zuma Wire/AP Images, 18; Adam Hunger/NCAA Photos/Getty Images, 23; G Fiume/Maryland Terrapins/Getty Images Sport/Getty Images, 25; G Fiume/NCAA Photos/ Getty Images, 28–29, 31; Andrew Katsampes/ISI Photos/Getty Images Sport/Getty Images, 34; Mitchell Layton/Getty Images Sport/Getty Images, 38; Lance King/Getty Images Sport/Getty Images, 43; Shutterstock Images, 44

Editor: Charlie Beattie
Series Designer: Jake Nordby

Library of Congress Control Number: 2021941598

Publisher's Cataloging-in-Publication Data

Names: Flynn, Brendan, author.
Title: Girls' Lacrosse / by Brendan Flynn
Description: Minneapolis, Minnesota : Abdo Publishing, 2022 | Series: Girls' SportsZone | Includes online resources and index.
Identifiers: ISBN 9781532196355 (lib. bdg.) | ISBN 9781098218164 (ebook)
Subjects: LCSH: Lacrosse--Juvenile literature. | Sports for girls--Juvenile literature. | Lacrosse for girls--Juvenile literature. | Team sports--Juvenile literature.
Classification: DDC 796.347--dc23

TABLE OF
CONTENTS

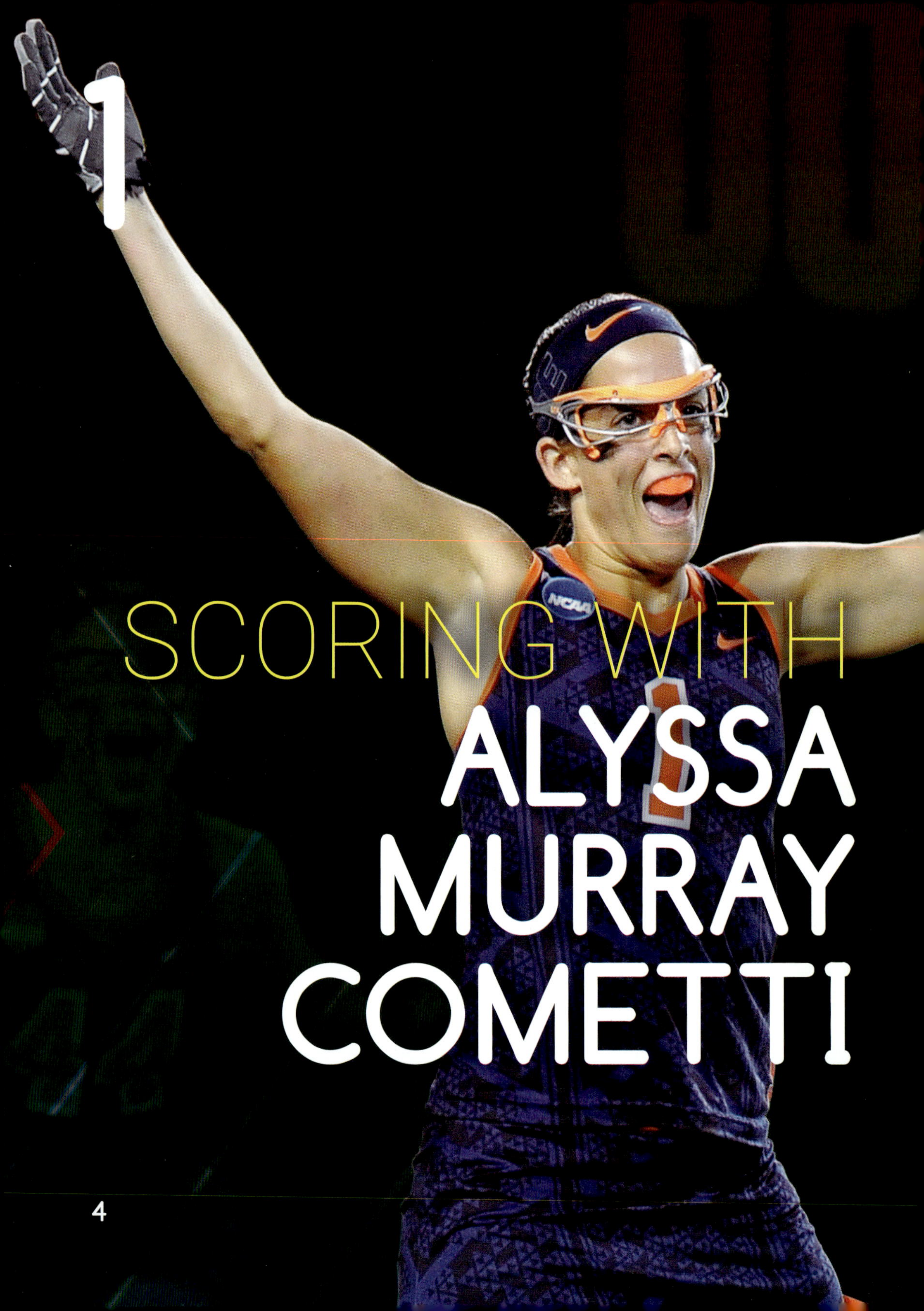

1

ALYSSA MURRAY COMETTI

No. 2-ranked Syracuse University was playing its final regular-season game of the 2014 schedule. The contest against No. 11 Loyola University Maryland was an important tune-up for the upcoming National Collegiate Athletic Association (NCAA) Tournament. It was also Senior Day, the final home game for the Orange's 10 seniors.

Attacker Alyssa Murray (now Alyssa Murray Cometti) was one of those seniors, and she wanted to make sure that she and her classmates finished on a high note. Murray scored two first-half goals and added four assists as Syracuse took a 7–5 lead into halftime.

Loyola came out fast in the second half. The Greyhounds scored five straight goals to take a 13–10 lead with 5:40 to play. That's when Murray came to the rescue.

The school's third all-time leading scorer carried the ball toward the right of Loyola's goal. A defender guarded her tightly, so Murray planted her foot and came to a quick stop. The move sent her opponent sprawling. Murray then made a full spin, faced the net, and fired a low shot that beat the goalie.

TEWAARATON AWARD

Since 2001 the Tewaaraton Award has been given to the top male and top female college lacrosse players in the country each season. The name comes from the Mohawk word for lacrosse, to honor the Iroquois people, commonly credited as the inventors of the game. Taylor Cummings of the University of Maryland is the only three-time winner of the award (2014–16). Through 2021, three other players had won it twice—Northwestern University's Kristen Kjellman (2006–07) and Hannah Nielsen (2008–09) and Maryland's Katie Schwarzmann (2012–13).

She was far from finished. One minute later, Murray found a seam in the Loyola defense. She charged through it, attacking the area directly in front of the net. A Loyola defender knocked her down with a high stick, but the falling Murray got off a low shot that found its way into the net.

With the momentum fully on their side, the Orange went on to tie the game in the final minute, then scored twice in overtime for a 15–13 victory.

In one short flurry, Murray showed what it takes to be a dynamic scorer—speed, quickness, strength, agility, and accuracy. Those skills served her well in her four years at

Murray fires a shot against Stony Brook University during the 2014 NCAA Tournament. She finished her senior year with 65 goals.

Syracuse. Murray was a two-time finalist for the Tewaaraton Award, given to the top player in college lacrosse. She was also a three-time first-team All-American and the first player in school history with three 100-point seasons. Murray helped

JEN ADAMS

Former Maryland star Jen Adams was one of the best offensive players the women's game has ever seen. The three-time All-American led the Terrapins to four straight national titles from 1998 to 2001. The Australian was named collegiate player of the year three times and won the first women's Tewaaraton Award in 2001. Through 2021, Adams was second on the NCAA's all-time scoring list with 445 points and seventh all-time with 267 goals.

Adams thrived on the international stage too. She played in three World Cups for Australia and served as team captain when the team won the championship in 2005. She was hired as the head coach at Loyola in 2009 and was inducted into the National Lacrosse Hall of Fame in 2012.

lead the Orange to the NCAA Final Four three straight seasons and played in two national championship games. She is the school's all-time leader in NCAA Tournament scoring with 33 goals in 11 games.

She accomplished all that even after tearing a knee ligament as a senior in high school. Murray had to spend the first part of her freshman year in college rebuilding strength in her knee and getting used to playing again. She refused to let the injury slow her down. Murray started every game as a freshman. As a sophomore, she led the nation in scoring with 74 goals and 105 points.

"Since she showed up on campus, she wanted to be the

best," Syracuse head coach Gary Gait said. "She worked at it every day."

Murray's goal totals dipped a bit her last two years, but that's because Kayla Treanor arrived to help carry the load in 2013. Treanor and Murray proved to be a dangerous one-two punch during their two seasons together in Syracuse. Treanor went on to score 260 career goals, which ranked sixth in NCAA history when she graduated in 2016. She credited much of that success to Murray.

"I think she's helped to change the culture of the program," Treanor said. "She makes everyone here better. Playing next to her, I think it's really helped me and improved my game."

Making a Play

Amazing offensive skills are on display during every lacrosse game. Courtney Murphy scored an NCAA-record 341 goals in her career at Stony Brook University, including a jaw-dropping 100 in 21 games in 2016. Boston College's Charlotte North broke that single-season record in 2021 with 102 goals, also in 21 games.

There are several keys to being a great attacker. One of the most important is having a hard and accurate shot. Shots aimed toward the corners of the net are usually harder for a goalie to save. Foot speed and the ability to change speeds

Boston College's Charlotte North fires home her record-setting 101st goal of the 2021 season during the NCAA championship game against Syracuse.

are also important. A well-timed stutter step or a quick, tricky move can help an attacker get by the defender. "As an offensive player, I'm at my best when my feet feel really light and quick, so I always put in a little extra time on box drills to work on turns and quick changes of direction," Murray said.

Another key is being able to successfully cradle the ball. Attackers should also be able to avoid stick checks by defenders. A stick check can knock the ball loose from the pocket of an attacker's stick. Location on the field is also important. An attacker needs to find spots where she is comfortable shooting.

QUICK TIP:
SHOOTING STYLES

There are four main shooting styles: overhand, sidearm, backhand, and bounce shots. The overhand shot is the most common and is usually the most effective. To practice this shot, position the head of the stick above your shoulder and even with your ear. When shooting, the best attackers transfer weight from their rear foot to their front foot. A strong wrist movement carries the shot. A sidearm shot provides more speed but less accuracy. A backhand shot can surprise the defense. Bounce shots are purposely aimed at the ground. This can cause problems for a goalie because she will not know how the ball will react after it bounces.

2

PASSING WITH
KYLIE OHLMILLER

Kylie Ohlmiller camped out behind the net with the ball. Moving back and forth on the balls of her feet, she looked for a teammate to break free from her defender.

Then, as she so often did, Ohlmiller spotted her Stony Brook University teammate Courtney Murphy in front of the net. With a flick of her wrists, Ohlmiller whipped a quick pass to Murphy, who made a clean catch. Murphy then made a couple of moves and fired a shot past the University of Maryland-Baltimore County goalie.

That was just the start of a huge day for Ohlmiller. Later in the first half, she took a pass on the right side of the net, darted across the face of the goal, and flicked a shot back over her shoulder for a goal. Ohlmiller's shot set the NCAA record for most points in a career.

In the second half, Ohlmiller made another sharp pass from behind the net. This time her sister, Taryn, was on the receiving end, and she buried another goal for Stony Brook.

Kylie Ohlmiller lines up a pass while playing for Stony Brook University.

HANNAH NIELSEN

Before Kylie Ohlmiller came along, many people considered Northwestern University's Hannah Nielsen the greatest passer in the history of women's lacrosse. In her senior year of 2009, Nielsen led the nation with 142 points. That is the fifth-highest single-season point total in NCAA history. Her 83 assists that year were an NCAA record until Ohlmiller passed her with 86 in 2017. Nielsen won her second straight Tewaaraton Award her senior year. On February 17, 2009, she became the first player to record 10 assists in one game. She held the career assists record with 224 before Ohlmiller broke it. Through 2021 they were the only players with 200 career assists.

That pass gave Ohlmiller another NCAA record—most assists in a career.

In four years at Stony Brook between 2015 and 2018, Ohlmiller amassed 498 points. That beat the previous NCAA record holder, Jen Adams, by 53. Ohlmiller's 246 assists topped the previous record by 22. It's no wonder she was a four-time All-American and a two-time Tewaaraton Award finalist. "Kylie's got great field vision," University of Maryland coach Cathy Reese said. "Not only is she a great shooter, but I think that what makes her so talented is the fact that she can see open people and hit those feeds."

Ohlmiller remained humble about her accomplishments. She credited players like Murphy for her success.

Hannah Nielsen (7) cradles the ball for Northwestern during the 2008 national championship game against the University of Pennsylvania. Nielsen's Wildcats won 10–6.

"Obviously, none of those things would have happened without the teammates that I had on the field," Ohlmiller said. "I wouldn't have the assist record without my teammates finishing the plays."

The best offensive players can both pass and shoot. Ohlmiller's ability to find the net on her own made her a matchup nightmare for defenders. They didn't know whether she was going to shoot or pass. And her creativity on the field created new ways to impact the game. "Her ability to throw behind-the-back passes is something the sport hasn't seen before," Murphy said. "If you guard her to dodge, she's going to feed. If you play her to feed, she dodges. There's so many different ways she can score."

Playing with creativity and instinct wasn't just an offensive strategy for Ohlmiller. She saw it mainly as a reminder to enjoy the game. "You're supposed to have fun with the game, so think outside the box when you're practicing and try new things," Ohlmiller said. "Ultimately, if you can throw a pass between your legs or around the back, then you're going to be able to throw a regular pass in a game. Not only that, but there are going to be opportunities to use those trick passes in real games, too. . . . If you have that tool in your toolbox, why not use it?"

SISTER ACT

Kylie Ohlmiller was a record setter at Stony Brook, but her younger sister, Taryn, wasn't far behind. She graduated in 2021 with impressive career totals of 219 goals, 194 assists, and 413 points. Her point total was third in NCAA history, trailing only those of her sister and Maryland's Jen Adams. Her total bumped former Stony Brook teammate Courtney Murphy to fourth place on that list.

Passing and Catching

The ability to move the ball around the field is important.

Ohlmiller tallied at least one point in 83 of her 84 career games at Stony Brook.

Goalies, defenders, and midfielders must make effective passes to work the ball into the attack zone. Passes also can come in fast-break situations. For example, in a two-on-one, an attacker can pass to a teammate when the defender or goalie is expecting a shot. Passes can be sent the full length across the field or downfield. Passes also can be sent from behind the opponent's net to an attacker.

Taryn Ohlmiller, Kylie's younger sister, had 56 assists during the 2021 season.

Even the most visionary passer will struggle without being fundamentally sound, however. Players such as Ohlmiller spend hours practicing the basics of passing and catching the ball.

It is most important that a pass be accurate. However, a harder-thrown pass has a better chance of reaching a teammate. If a pass is too slow or is lobbed high in the air, an opposing player will have more time to get in position to make an interception. The most effective pass is an overhand pass. This is when the stick travels from high to low as the pass is made.

Receiving a ball is also important. The receiver should make herself a good target for a pass. This means lining up the face of the pocket to the passer. A receiver should keep the pocket of her stick above her shoulder and keep the stick upright. She should establish space between herself and opposing players. Once the ball lands in the pocket, it is important to immediately cradle the ball to keep possession.

Players do not have to be at practice to work on their passing and receiving. Two friends can practice throwing to each other in standing positions or on the run. In a game, most passing situations will occur while running.

QUICK TIP:
PASS AND RECEIVE

To practice passing all you need are a few lacrosse balls and a teammate. Face each other about 10 yards (9.1 m) apart. Practice overhand passing and receiving. Once you can do that well, turn your body so that it is sideways to your teammate. Again, practice the throws. As the passing gets better, try moving farther back while still passing accurately.

3
GOALKEEPING WITH
MEGAN TAYLOR

The top-ranked Maryland Terrapins faced No. 2 Boston College (BC) in the 2019 NCAA championship game. Maryland had won the title three times in the previous five years, while BC had come up one game short two years in a row. Maryland goalie Megan Taylor did her best to make sure both trends continued.

With the Terrapins leading 4–2 in the first half, Taylor came up big. Sam Apuzzo, Boston College's reigning Tewaaraton Award winner, had a free-position shot at the 8-meter arc in front of the net. Apuzzo led the nation with 94 goals that year. Taylor took a strong position in front of the net. Her feet were shoulder-width apart, her knees bent, and her stick held high. She was ready for whatever type of shot Apuzzo might attempt.

Apuzzo aimed a hard shot over Taylor's shoulder, but Maryland's senior goalie snagged it out of the air, denying Boston College a chance to cut into the lead. Not long after,

Megan Taylor sets herself in the Maryland goal during the 2019 NCAA Tournament.

Boston College's other Tewaaraton finalist, Dempsey Arsenault, received a pass in front of the goal. She had an open shot, but Taylor reacted quickly to deflect it over the net.

THE BEST, AND BUSIEST, OF ALL TIME

Many goalkeepers have won multiple championships and set records. Morgan Lathrop set a school record at Northwestern with 553 saves. She started 86 games and won 83. Dana Robinson made 320 saves for Towson University in 1983. That was the highest single-season total in NCAA history. But through 2021, only one player in NCAA women's history had more than 1,000 career saves. Chris Lindsey, who played at Georgetown University from 1995 to 1998, totaled 1,067 saves, 99 more than any other goalie.

Taylor stopped seven first-half shots as Maryland took an 8–4 halftime lead. The Terrapins held on in the second half, pulling out a 12–10 victory for the program's record-setting fourteenth NCAA title. It was Taylor's second championship—she also was in the net as Maryland defeated BC 16–13 in the 2017 title game. As usual, she received high praise for her play. "She was fantastic and made some unbelievable saves to anchor our defense, which I think played the best that it has all season, especially against an offense that's as high-scoring as Boston College has been this year," said Maryland head coach Cathy Reese.

Morgan Lathrop drops to a knee to stop a shot in Northwestern's 7–4 victory over Dartmouth College in the 2006 NCAA championship game.

Taylor made history that season, becoming the first goalie, male or female, ever to win the Tewaaraton Award. In 2020 she was the first lacrosse player ever to be named a finalist for the James E. Sullivan Award, which honors the top amateur athlete in the United States. She also has been part of the US national team since 2017.

The Final Line of Defense

In a traditional lacrosse game, seven field players are allowed in the defensive zone. The goalkeeper is the last line of defense behind them. Lacrosse is a fast-moving, high-scoring game. Shutouts are rare, but a good goalkeeper can make a huge difference, especially in close games. The goalkeeper needs to stop as many shots as possible and then clear the ball to a teammate to start a counterattack.

Only the goalkeeper, or her deputy, may occupy the space inside the 8.5-foot (2.6-m) goal circle. Any other defender or attacker who crosses the line is subject to a goal-circle foul. That isolation makes a goalie's technique and positioning especially important, because no defenders can block a close-range shot. A goalkeeper should keep the head of her stick upright and maintain a strong stance. Better positioning gives the attacker

FABULOUS FRANKIE CARIDI

After a year at Division II powerhouse Adelphi University in Garden City, New York, Frankie Caridi transferred to nearby Stony Brook University, a Division I school. Caridi did more than handle the jump up in competition. In her first season, in 2013, she led the nation in both save percentage (.530) and goals-against average (5.71). In 2014, her senior year, she led both categories again. Through 2021, six goalkeepers had led the nation in both categories in the same year, but only Caridi had done it twice.

Taylor stops a shot from Northwestern's Lauren Gilbert during the 2019 NCAA tournament semifinals.

less open space at which to aim. Goalies should shift their bodies to stay in line with the attacker.

A goalkeeper has different equipment than field players. One big difference is the stick. A goalkeeper's stick has a bigger pocket. The larger pocket helps to stop or block shots. Composite sticks are ideal because they are lighter than wood sticks and easier to control. Goalkeepers also have more protective equipment than field players. This includes a helmet,

Stony Brook's Frankie Caridi looks to pass during a 2014 NCAA Tournament game against Syracuse.

a chest protector, a throat protector, goalie gloves, and leg padding.

Goalies are relied upon to provide stability for the team. No lacrosse goalkeeper can stop every shot. The key for the goalie is to always be ready for the next challenge, no matter what happened before. A goalie cannot get rattled, according to Northwestern coach Kelly Amonte Hiller. A goalie must reset quickly after a goal is scored.

Former Loyola goalkeeper Tricia Dabrowski agrees. "If a team scores on you two or three times in a row, it's easy to falter," Dabrowski said. "A great goalie can bounce back from that and learn to separate their mistakes from the mistakes of their teammates. Remember, the ball's got to get through eleven other players to get to you."

Amonte Hiller said a great way for goalkeepers to practice is to face tennis balls from close range. A coach or teammate uses an attacker's stick to throw tennis balls toward the cage from just a few yards away. The goalkeeper must attempt to step up and knock the ball away with the shaft of her stick, not the pocket. Using tennis balls helps develop quick hand-eye coordination.

QUICK TIP:
MAKING SAVES

Fundamentals are key. When facing an attack, the goalie should keep her stick flat to the shooter and her hands and elbows in front of her body. Positioning is important too. If an attacker goes behind the net with the ball, the goalie should remain in front of the net with her stick up. She should be ready to move quickly to the post when the attacker comes around to that side. To practice, get help from some teammates. Have them stand several yards away in a semicircle facing the net. Then have each player take turns shooting. This will help give the goalie a feel for positioning and where to stand for shots that come from different angles.

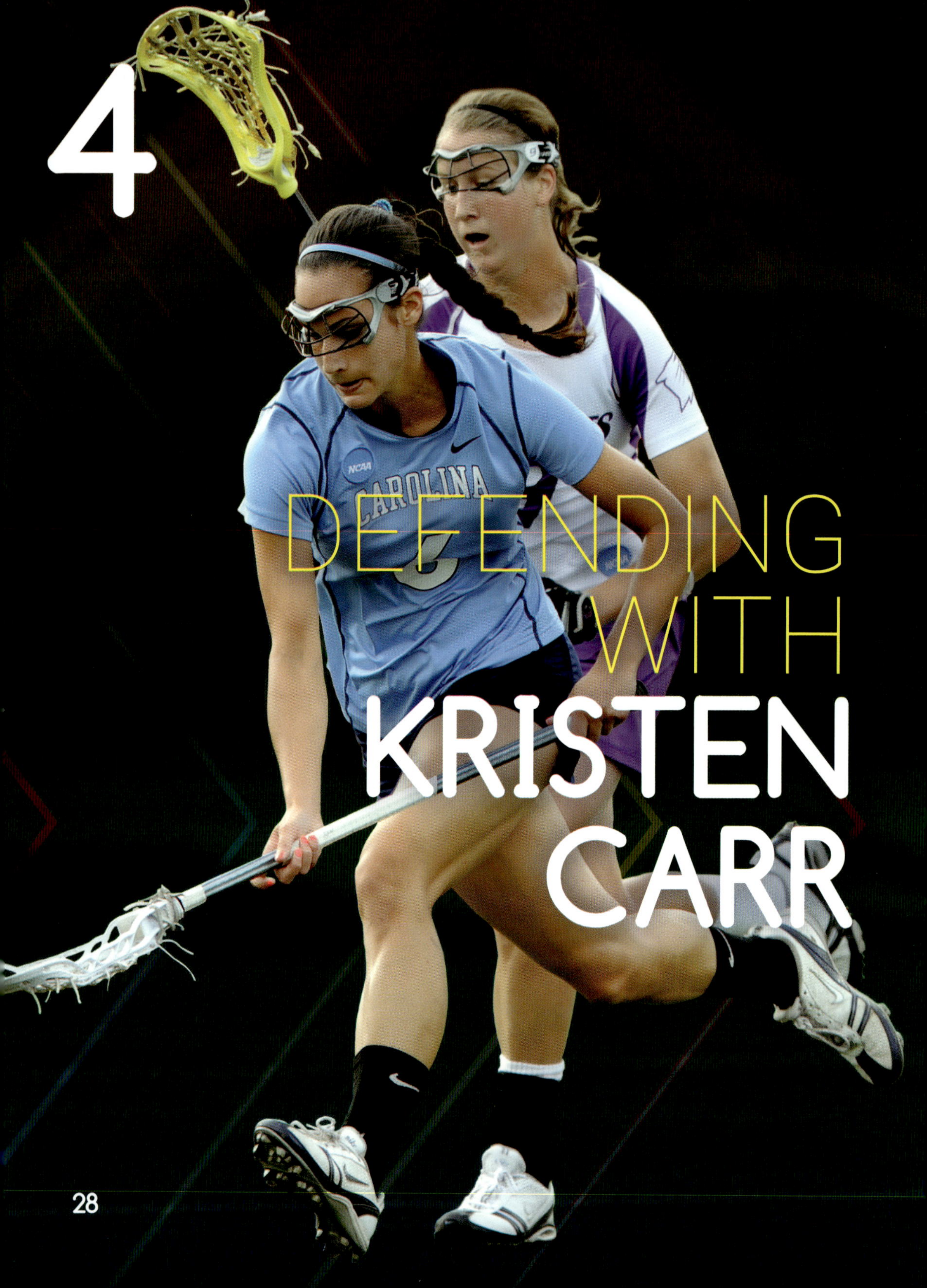

4
DEFENDING WITH
KRISTEN CARR

Kristen Carr is a longtime starting defender on the US national team. She also has played in the Women's Professional Lacrosse League and has coached at several powerhouse college programs. She is one of the greatest players in US lacrosse history. But if you mention "Kristen Carr" to lacrosse players and fans, they might not immediately know whom you're talking about. That's because she's primarily known by a nickname she picked up on her soccer team when she was five years old—Cookie.

"Most people think it's because I love desserts and sweets," Carr said with a laugh. "But really, I guess I was super aggressive as a kid and just had such a nose for the ball and always wanted to take the ball away from my attacker. So they started calling me a 'tough little cookie,' and as the years grew on and I got older, 'Cookie' just stuck."

That mentality helped Carr build a reputation as a strong defender. She began playing for her country in 2008, when she was still two years away from finishing her college career at the University of North Carolina. At 5 feet, 10 inches tall, she towers over many opposing attackers. She also has quick feet and a willingness to mix it up with anyone.

"Her presence alone is really intimidating to an attacker," Carr's US teammate Lindsey Munday said. "She has great size, she has great power, and along with that she's really smart. I think she uses her body really well, and she's really physical. It's not just one thing or the other; she sort of has it all as a defender. She's really tough, she's really feisty. We're just thankful she's on our team."

Carr was a regular starter for the US team that won the gold medal at the 2013 World Cup. The Americans did it again four years later, with Carr leading a defense that allowed just 4.2 goals per game in pool play. Carr played a big role

THE BEST AT TURNOVERS

Moira Muthig's standout year in 2000 has never been equaled. Muthig was a defender at Manhattan College in New York City. That year she caused an NCAA record 82 turnovers in just 14 games. Georgetown University's Michi Ellers was the first to top 200 career caused turnovers. She finished with 204, a record that stood until 2016, when Wagner College's Shea Gegan ended her career with 235. Ellers went on to play with the US national team and coach at Georgetown.

in both of those tournament victories thanks to her unique defensive skills.

"I think it's rare to have her tools, to play with the physicality she plays with and the finesse at the same time," former US coach Ricky Fried said. "We want to play a fast, aggressive game and we want to dictate to our opponent whether we're on offense or defense, and she's someone who can do that."

Causing Turnovers

A defender cannot wait for the play to come to her. She must take on an attacker through positioning and quickness. While bodychecking is legal in the men's game, it is not allowed in women's lacrosse. Too much physical play will draw a whistle from the referee. Stick checking is not fully allowed until a player reaches the high school level.

The job of every defender includes causing turnovers, intercepting passes, and picking up ground balls. Once a defender has the ball, she must protect it long enough to find an open midfielder or attacker for a pass.

Defenders communicate with each other and the goalkeeper constantly. Sometimes attackers will change positions to cross up defenders. The defensive players might need to switch marks. One defender might yell out "switch" to alert another.

CHRISTY FINCH

Christy Finch was one of the top defenders in NCAA history. She helped lead Northwestern to national championships in all four of her years with the Wildcats. Her 70 caused turnovers in 2008 led the nation. She totaled 183 in her collegiate career, ranking seventh all-time in the NCAA through 2021. In addition, she was the 2008 national defender of the year and a two-time All-American. Following her playing career, Finch went on to become an assistant coach at Ohio State University before taking over as the head coach at Stetson University in Florida in 2014.

Christy Finch, *right*, won four national titles in four years as a standout defender for Northwestern.

This can prevent other teams from finding open areas to attack. Defenders must prevent breakaways on the goalkeeper and know when to take on the shooter in a two-on-one break. These instincts come from years of practice and guidance from coaches.

Temple University's Belle Mastropietro, *right*, defends against Boston College's Cassidy Weeks during a 2021 NCAA Tournament game.

Northwestern coach and former US national team star Kelly Amonte Hiller said the sliding concept is key in defending properly. Sliding is the technical name for backing up a teammate. If one defender is beaten, another defender slides from her position into the open space to help. Coaches introduce this concept as players get more advanced.

Seven defenders, including the goalkeeper, are allowed on the defensive side of the field. Each is responsible for one of the seven attackers allowed in the offensive zone.

Defenders may use longer sticks than other players. But before adopting a longer stick, a player should make sure it is a good fit. A player is better off using a stick that is shorter and can be held properly than a longer stick on which she needs to choke up.

QUICK TIP:
PICKING A SIDE

The key for a defender is always keeping herself between the attacker and the net. Then she needs to recognize which direction the attacker wants to go. To achieve this, watch the attacker's eyes. This can provide a big hint as to where the attacker is headed. Also notice which hand is at the top of her stick. If an attacker has her right hand at the top, then she is likely to go toward her right and shoot that way. A lefty is more likely to go left. A good drill to practice takes just one teammate. The attacker has the ball and sets up with her back to the net. The defender stands a few yards in front. When the play begins, the attacker will attempt to go right or left, and then shoot. The defender should practice staying in front of that attacker, moving side to side. The goal is to force a bad shot and maybe even a turnover. Practice this against both left-handers and right-handers.

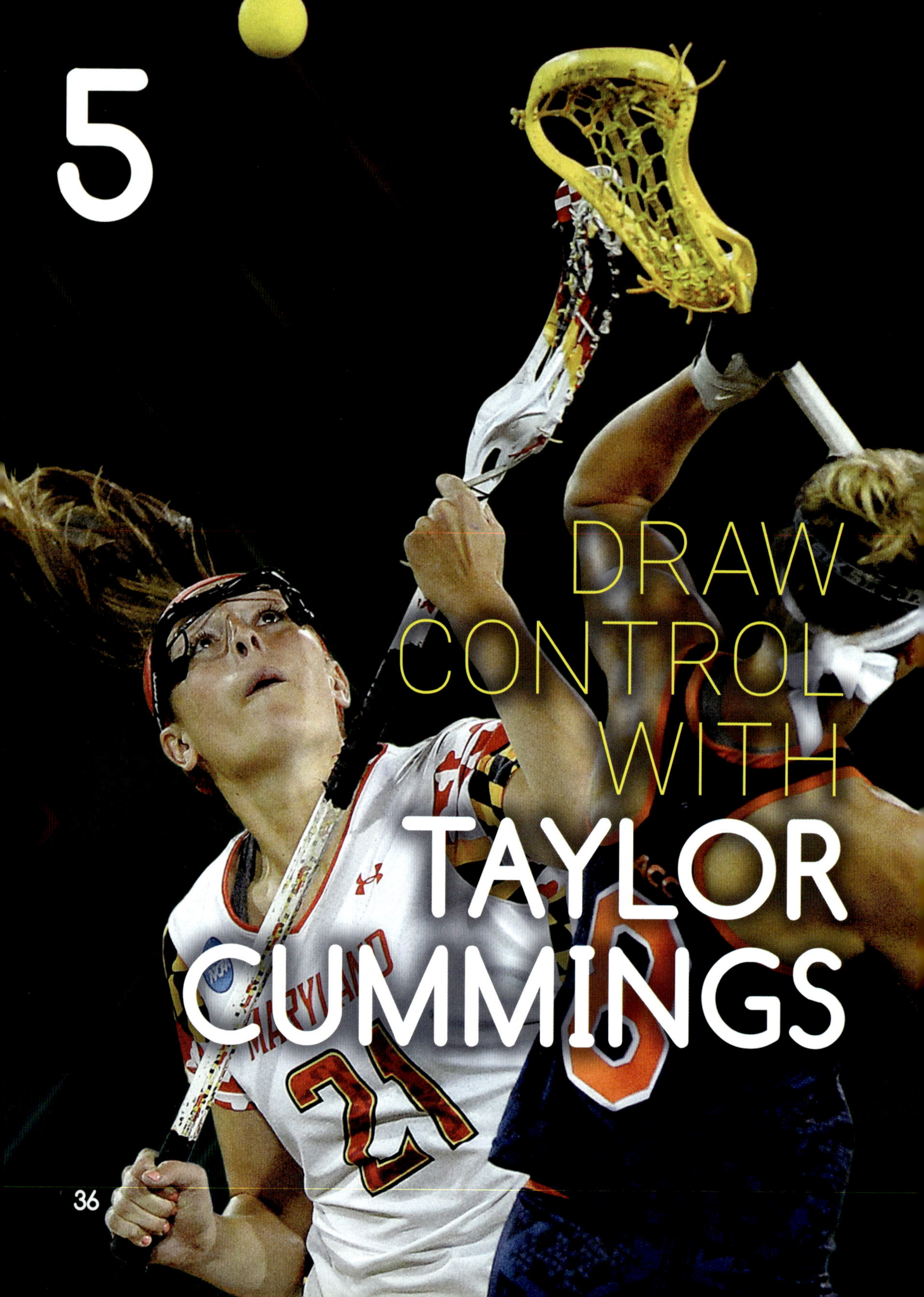

5
DRAW CONTROL WITH
TAYLOR CUMMINGS
36

Taylor Cummings left the University of Maryland in 2016 with quite the winning legacy. The Terrapins went 88–4 in her four years on campus and won two national titles. Cummings won the Tewaaraton Award three times—the only player to do that.

Cummings was accustomed to winning in a different sense. She was dominant in the draw circle, the area that determines which team gets to start on offense at the start of each half or after a goal. She holds the Maryland school record with 509 career draw controls, which was sixth in NCAA history through 2021.

"In close games, [draw controls] can make or break a game," Cummings said after posting a career-high 13 of them in a game against Rutgers University during her senior year. "When you win the draw, you kind of get a momentum going. If we can score and win the draw, that can build a lot of confidence in a young group like we have."

Maryland's Taylor Cummings, *left*, battles for a draw against Syracuse's Kirkland Locey during the 2014 NCAA championship game.

Cummings (21) leaps to snag the ball out of the air after a draw against Rutgers in April 2015.

The four-time All-American led the Terrapins in draw controls in each of her four seasons. She broke the school's all-time single-season records with 144 draw controls and 52 caused turnovers in 2016. Her totals in ground balls, draw controls, and caused turnovers increased every year from her freshman through senior seasons.

All those draw controls led to greater time of possession for Maryland, and that led to more scoring opportunities for Cummings and her teammates. "It's so crucial for [Cummings] to get us going," former teammate Alice Mercer said. "She's always working for the next draw. And I think that's what makes her such a special, dominant player."

That's just one of the many reasons that Maryland coach Cathy Reese had such high praise after Cummings accepted her third straight Tewaaraton Award. "You guys see it. She's just so fun to watch. She's electric," Reese said. "She's passionate, she's a great leader, she takes care of business all over the field."

KRISTEN KJELLMAN

Three-time All-American and former US national team star midfielder Kristen Kjellman credits her strong stick skills for her success. Kjellman won three straight NCAA titles with Northwestern. She was the first lacrosse player, man or woman, to win the Tewaaraton Trophy in consecutive seasons.

Kjellman finished her college career as the NCAA all-time leader in draw controls with 268, then she continued that domination in the center circle for the national team. She had a team-high 20 draw controls at the 2009 World Cup. Kjellman retired from international play in 2011.

Center Circle Draw

Draws are important for one simple reason: they determine possession of the ball. The lacrosse draw is like a face-off in ice hockey. If a team gets the ball, it can try to score. Winning draws is a good way to ensure that a team gets more possessions and more chances to score. "If you don't win the draw, you can't have more opportunities on the offense," said Gary Gait, the Syracuse women's lacrosse coach who won three men's national titles with Syracuse as a player.

"In lacrosse, it's a lot harder to get back possession," former Temple University attacker Maddie Gebert said. "Once you have possession, you kind of control the game."

There are several draws in each lacrosse game. There is always a draw to start the game and at the beginning of the second half. In addition, there

MIX IT UP

The player in the center circle can only do so much on a draw. The players around the edge of the circle must do their part too. Northwestern coach Kelly Amonte Hiller, one of the best at draw controls during her playing days, teaches her players to spread out to different areas of the field during a draw. This allows a team to cover more space and have a better chance to possess the ball. Amonte Hiller said deception can be used to fool an opponent. She tells her players to start out in a different space from where they will end up.

Cummings scored at least 60 goals in three of her four seasons at Maryland.

is a draw after each goal. A 15–14 game, for example, would have 31 draws.

For a draw, one player from each team lines up facing her draw opponent inside the center circle. Four players from each team stand around the edge of the circle. The two players in the middle hold their sticks horizontally at waist-high level with the pockets facing in. The referee then places the ball between the two sticks in the back of each basket. The two sticks push together to hold the ball. When the whistle sounds, the players immediately try to get their stick under the ball to fling it up in the air toward a teammate. Strength and quick stick skills are important to winning draws.

"For the draw, it's basically the grittiness and having trust in your draw taker," former Temple defender Kara Nakrasius said. "You have to be prepared beforehand. It takes a lot of extra work, and it's important to get that good relationship with everyone else in the circle."

QUICK TIP:
CRADLING

Cradling the ball in the pocket of the stick is the way a player maintains possession. Kelly Amonte Hiller compares cradling in lacrosse to dribbling in basketball or stickhandling in ice hockey. She says a player should maintain a triple-threat position, from which a player can either run with the ball, pass, or shoot. When cradling, always face the target and never stand still. A stationary player who is cradling creates a vulnerability that a defender could exploit. Amonte Hiller says players should keep their arms away from the body while cradling and protect their stick from defenders.

Shelby Fredericks, *left*, of Northwestern and Duke University's Ellie Majure face off during a 2016 game.

Her coach, Bonnie Rosen, added, "Becoming a great draw player is really about deciding you actually want to get good at something. It's one of those things, if you put the time in and you study your craft, you can get really good."

Cummings advises young players in the draw circle to keep their top hand close to the head of the stick to increase power and control. She also suggests keeping an eye on the referee to sense when she's ready to blow the whistle.

FIELD
DIAGRAM

ARC AND FAN

The women's field includes markings for an 8-meter arc and a 12-meter fan. The arc and fan are used to determine fouls and positioning after major fouls are whistled.

CENTER CIRCLE

This is where the draws are held to begin a half or restart play after a goal. The center circle has a radius of 30 feet (9.1 m).

GOAL CIRCLE

This is a circle with a radius of 8.5 feet (2.6 m). Only the goalkeeper, or her deputy, may be inside the goal circle.

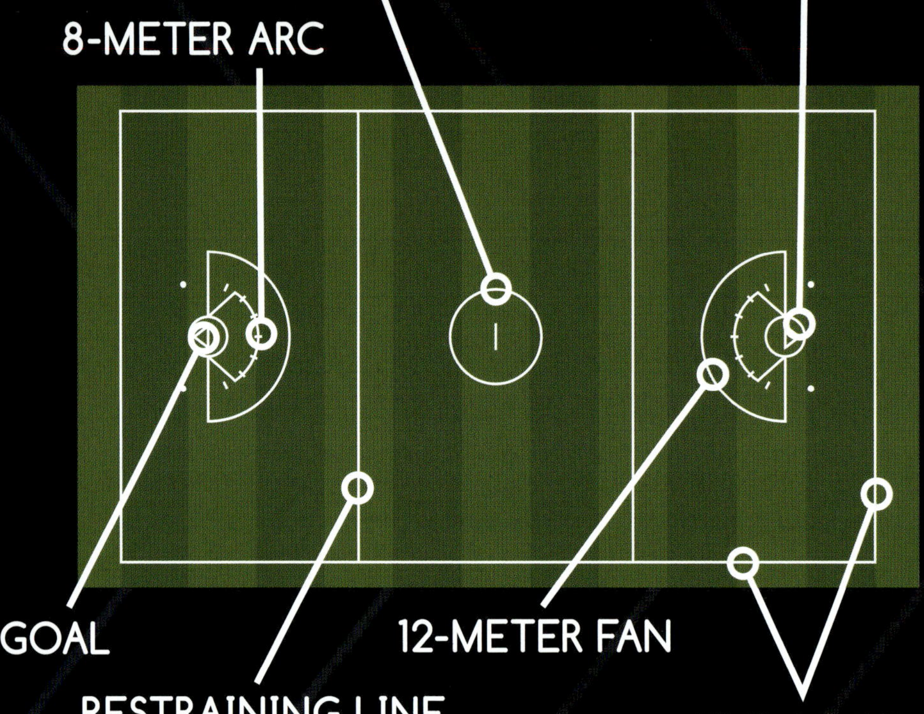

RESTRAINING LINE

This is the line that separates one group of players from another. Only seven defenders, a goalkeeper, and seven attackers may be inside the restraining line on either side of the field.

END LINES AND SIDELINES

These lines form the boundary of a lacrosse field.

GLOSSARY

amateur
A person who plays a sport without getting paid.

assist
A pass that leads directly to a goal.

attacker
Also called a forward, a player usually located in a team's offensive end trying to score goals.

cradle
To hold the ball in the pocket of a lacrosse stick while running.

deputy
A designated defender who is allowed to enter the goal circle when her goalie leaves the circle.

dodge
A deceptive move designed to create space for an attacker against a defender.

draw
A face-off between two opposing players inside the center circle.

feed
Another term for passing the ball.

ground ball
When the ball falls from the stick pocket to the ground.

midfielder
A player who is responsible for playing both offense and defense.

points
A statistic that combines a player's totals of both goals and assists.

stutter step
A step used to confuse an opponent. A player will go in one direction, change speed with her feet, and then accelerate again.

turnover
When one team loses possession of the ball to the other team.

MORE
INFORMATION

BOOKS

Bowker, Paul D. *Total Lacrosse*. Minneapolis, MN: Abdo, 2017.

Myers, Jess. *Make Me the Best Lacrosse Player*. Minneapolis, MN: Abdo, 2017.

ONLINE RESOURCES

To learn more about women's lacrosse, please visit **abdobooklinks.com** or scan this QR code. These links are routinely monitored and updated to provide the most current information available.

PLACES TO
VISIT

Reverend Harold Ridley, S.J., Athletic Complex

2221 West Cold Spring Lane
Baltimore, MD 21211
410-617-1420
loyolagreyhounds.com/facilities/ridley-athletic
-complex/2

Ridley Athletic Complex, which is located on the Loyola Maryland campus in lacrosse-crazed Baltimore, is one of the premier college lacrosse stadiums in the country. It was built in 2010 to house the university's lacrosse and soccer teams.

The US Lacrosse Museum & National Hall of Fame

2 Loveton Circle
Sparks, MD 21152
410-235-6882, ext. 122
usalacrosse.com/national-lacrosse-hall-fame-and
-museum

This museum and hall of fame honors the history of lacrosse along with its greatest players and contributors. Artifacts, memorabilia, and art spanning from the Native American origins of lacrosse through today are featured. The Hall of Fame Gallery has interactive information about the hall of famers who have had the greatest impact on the sport. The museum features a multimedia show and a documentary about lacrosse.

INDEX

ABOUT THE AUTHOR

Brendan Flynn is a San Francisco resident and an author of numerous children's books.